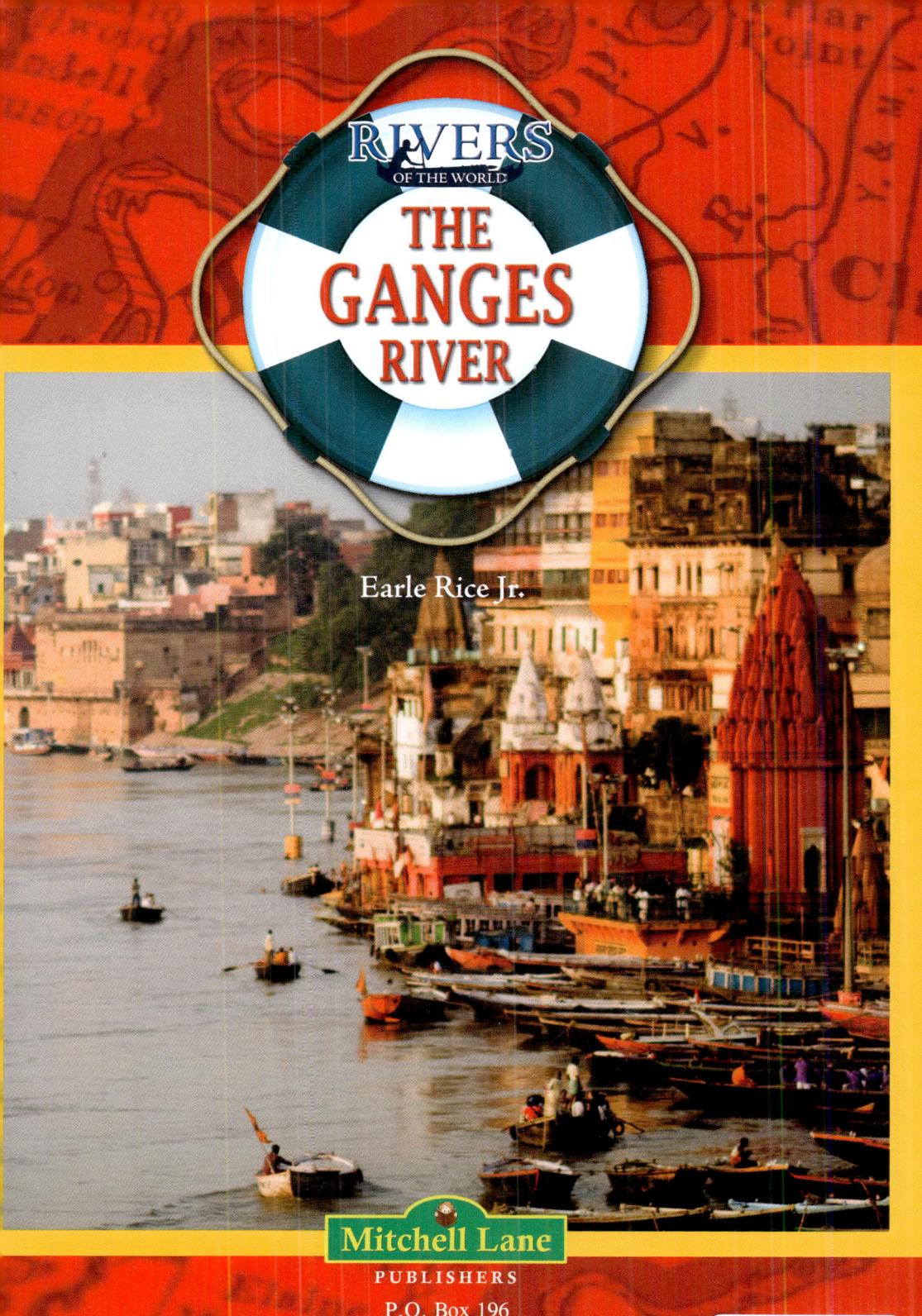

RIVERS
OF THE WORLD

THE GANGES RIVER

Earle Rice Jr.

Mitchell Lane
PUBLISHERS

P.O. Box 196
Hockessin, Delaware 19707

RIVERS
OF THE WORLD

The Amazon River
The Nile River
The Ganges River
The Mississippi River
The Rhine River
The Tigris (Euphrates) River
The Yangtze River
The Volga River

Copyright © 2013 by Mitchell Lane Publishers

Printing 1 2 3 4 5 6 7 8 9

All rights reserved. No part of this book may be reproduced without written permission from the publisher. Printed and bound in the United States of America.

PUBLISHER'S NOTE: The facts on which the story in this book is based have been thoroughly researched. Documentation of such research can be found on page 45. While every possible effort has been made to ensure accuracy, the publisher will not assume liability for damages caused by inaccuracies in the data, and makes no warranty on the accuracy of the information contained herein.

Library of Congress
Cataloging-in-Publication Data
Rice, Earle.
  The Ganges river / By Earle Rice Jr.
    p. cm.—(Rivers of the world)
  Includes bibliographical references and index.
  ISBN 978-1-61228-295-4 (library bound)
  1. Ganges River—Juvenile literature. I. Title.
DS485.G25R48 2012
954'.1—dc23
                                    2012009462

eBook ISBN: 9781612283685

PLB

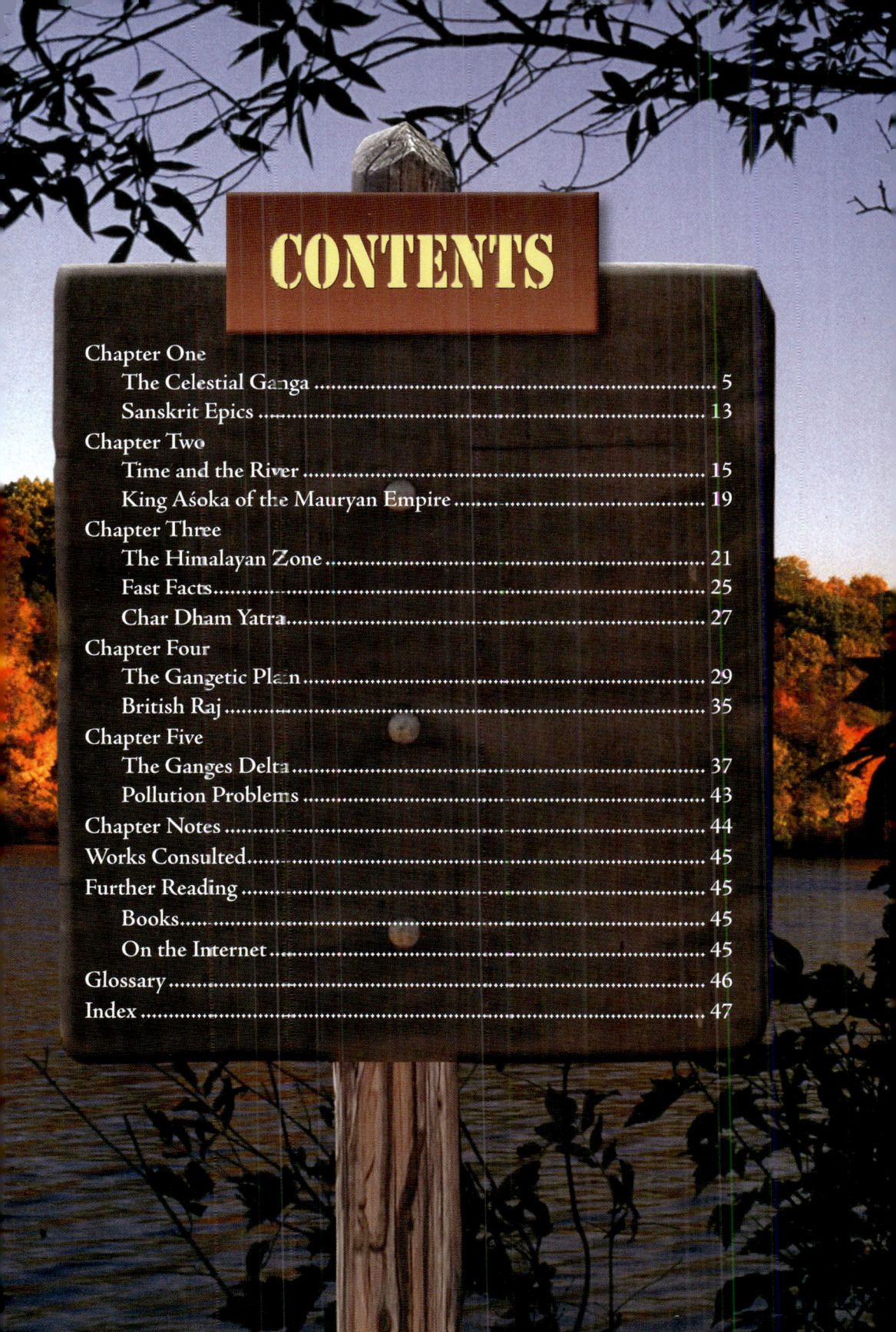

CONTENTS

Chapter One
   The Celestial Ganga 5
   Sanskrit Epics 13

Chapter Two
   Time and the River 15
   King Aśoka of the Mauryan Empire 19

Chapter Three
   The Himalayan Zone 21
   Fast Facts 25
   Char Dham Yatra 27

Chapter Four
   The Gangetic Plain 29
   British Raj 35

Chapter Five
   The Ganges Delta 37
   Pollution Problems 43

Chapter Notes 44
Works Consulted 45
Further Reading 45
   Books 45
   On the Internet 45
Glossary 46
Index 47

Boat ride on the Ganges

CHAPTER 1

The Celestial Ganga

"The Ganga has been a symbol of India's age-long culture and civilization, ever-changing, ever-flowing, and yet ever the same Ganga," noted Jawaharlal Nehru, India's first prime minister. "She reminds me of the Himalayas' snow-covered peaks and the deep valleys which I have loved so much, and the rich and vast plains below where my life and work have been cast."[1] A half billion Hindus call the Ganges River *Ganga Ma*, or Mother Ganges. They consider her sacred and think of her as their Mother Goddess.

The story of Ganga's birth goes back many centuries before the Common Era. At first, storytellers preserved her tale, passing it along orally from generation to generation. Much like the river itself, her creation myth took on many twists and turns, as it wended its way through the years. By the time Ganga's devotees learned to write, several different tales had emerged.

Each account of Ganga's creation claimed to be the one true version. All versions declare that Ganga

CHAPTER 1

Ganga, the River Goddess, is the only living goddess among the gods officially recognized by Hindus. They believe she descended to earth to rinse away the sins of humankind. The Holy Ganges is the earthly embodiment of the Goddess Ganga and represents her pristine coolness, piety, and purity.

was raised in the heavens by Brahma, the creator god. Beyond this common thread, Ganga's creation myths differ vastly. Adding to the confusion, Hindu scribes recorded all known versions of the *avatarana*, or the descent of the Ganges from heaven to earth.

The most popular version of the *avatarana* involves Shiva, the third god in the Hindu trinity. The trinity consists of Brahma, the god of creation; Vishnu, the preserver god; and Shiva, the god of destruction and regeneration. This version is told and retold in the *Mahabharata*

The Celestial Ganga

and the *Ramayana*, the two major Sanskrit epic poems of India. It is also told in several Puranas, which are Sanskrit verse texts relating mythological accounts of ancient days.

Shiva statue at Nageshwar

The story begins with a renowned sage of antiquity called Kapila. Kapila lived during the late 7th or early 6th century BCE. Buddhists connect him geographically to Kapilavastu, the birthplace of Buddha. Legend and contradiction surround him. He is said to have lived since the beginning of creation as the grandson of Brahma, and as an incarnation of both Vishnu and Agni, the god of fire.

One day, according to the *Mahabharata*, Kapila was disturbed while meditating by the 60,000 sons of a king named Sagara. Enraged by the interruption, the sage reduced Sagara's sons to ashes with a fiery gaze from his third eye. Kapila sent their ashes to the netherworld (the

CHAPTER 1

underworld, or world of the dead). Only the purifying waters of Ganga could bring salvation to the dead sons. But the river goddess resided in heaven and was unreachable. The souls of Sagara's sons, lacking their final rites, were thereby forced to wander the netherworld as ghosts.

Many years later, King Bhagirath, the great-great-grandson of Sagara, decided to seek salvation for his ancestors. He prayed to Brahma to send Ganga to earth so that she might release their souls. Brahma answered his prayers. He instructed Ganga to descend to earth and proceed to the nether regions. Her mission was to cleanse the ashes of Bhagirath's ancestors. Ganga plunged to earth with a force so violent that her waters threatened to sweep away the Earth. Bhagirath instantly prayed to Shiva for help.

Shiva reacted quickly. He rushed from his abode on Mount Kailas and broke Ganga's fall in his wild, matted hair. Gathering her cascading waters in his tangled locks, he released them as gentle streams across the mountains.

Brahma

The Celestial Ganga

Mount Kailas. Located in western Tibet, the mountain rises to a height of 21,778 feet (6,638 meters).

Shiva's touch graced Ganga with further sanctity. Using her energized powers, she created a different stream to remain on Earth.

The waiting King Bhagirath met Ganga in the Himalayas. He escorted her down into the plains to Haridwar, across the plains to the confluence with the Yamuna River at Allahabad, on to Varanasi, and finally to Ganga Sagar at the Bay of Bengal. Ganga descended to the netherworld, where she found the sons of Sagara and at long last released their souls.

Ganga and King Bhagirath often stopped to rest on their long journey from the mountains to the sea. Today, Hindus revere their resting places as sacred. Many travel to them on religious pilgrimages. To honor Bhagirath's pivotal role in the *avatarana* tale, the source stream of the Ganges in the Himalayas is named Bhagirathi, which is

Alaknanda and Bhagirathi meeting to form the Ganges

Sanskrit for "of Bhagirath." And so ends the creation myth of Ganga, the Mother Goddess of the Ganges.

Hindus believe Ganga to be the daughter of Himavat, king of the Himalayas, and his consort, the nymph Mena. They portray Ganga as voluptuous and beautiful. In their vision of her, she carries a pot overflowing with abundant life and fertility. She nourishes and sustains the universe. "She has become one of the most venerated deities [gods] in Hinduism," writes author and photographer Jon Nicholson, "and the Ganges is the most sacred of all rivers. Bathing in the river's waters brings deliverance from sins committed in the present and in all lives past."[2]

CHAPTER 1

Every year, millions of pilgrims visit the ancient city of Varanasi to bathe and wash away their sins in the Ganges at the Dasasvamedha Ghat. Adjacent to the bathing ghats are the famous burning ghats where as many as 40,000 bodies are cremated annually.

Hindus use its waters in ceremonies for purification. They administer *gangajal,* or Ganga water, to dying people in the waning moments of their lives for deliverance of their souls. The Ganges draws millions of pilgrims to its banks each year. The *Mahabharata* hails it as "the ultimate place of pilgrimage."[3] Those who bathe in it purify seven descendants. True believers come to be blessed or to celebrate religious events or rituals. Some come simply to die and have their ashes scattered upon the river's sacred waters.

Because Ganga descended from heaven, Hindus believe the Ganges is the only river to flow in all three worlds—heaven, earth, and the netherworld. The *Mahabharata* accordingly declares: "Here is the celestial river, sacred and sanctifying the three worlds. It is called the celestial Ganga. Plunging into it, you will attain your proper place."[4]

Sanskrit Epics

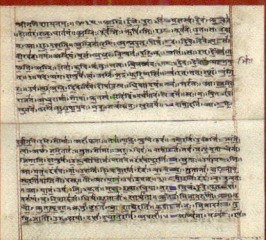

Rig Veda Sanskrit

Sanskrit is the classical literary language of Hinduism, the oldest of the world's major religions. Several of India's greatest epics are written in Sanskrit. Three principal works of Hinduism are the *Rig Veda* (or *Rigveda*), the *Mahabharata*, and the *Ramayana*.

The *Rig Veda* is the oldest scripture in the world. It is the most revered of the Vedas, the sacred hymns and verses of Hinduism. Composed of more than a thousand hymns to multiple gods, it offers insight into a great deal of Indian thought. Many scholars view its study as essential to understanding India.

Considered the foremost source on Indian civilization, the *Mahabharata* is a work of eighteen volumes. It ranks as the longest poem in world literature. Probably written by the sage Vyasa between 200 BCE and 200 CE, it comprises 100,000 verses. Primarily, it narrates an amazing account of competing dynasties and a great civil war in the kingdom of Kurukshetra. It also contains the *Bhagavad-Gita*, a religious classic of Hinduism. Its theme focuses on spiritual wisdom and attaining union with God through selfless action, knowledge, and devotion.

The *Ramayana* relates the story of Rama. He is dethroned by trickery and exiled with his wife, Sita. She is later abducted by a demon king. Rama allies himself with Sugriva, a monkey king, and Hanuman, a monkey general. Together, they defeat the demon king in a great battle at Lanka (modern-day Sri Lanka). Rama frees Sita and regains his throne.

The Ganges as it flows through the Kashmir valley in India in the shadow of the Himalayas

CHAPTER 2

Time and the River

About 100 million years before Ganga made her mythical plunge from Heaven, the Earth's surface was undergoing enormous changes. Its outer layer, or crust, had split into separate pieces and was floating on an underlying sea of molten rock. One of those pieces was the future subcontinent of India. It separated from southern Africa and shifted northeastward in a slow process called continental drift.

Over a time span of 40 to 50 million years, this shifting piece eventually collided with Asia. The colliding edges of the two landmasses turned skyward to form the jagged peaks of the Himalayas. This collision also joined the Indian subcontinent to Asia. Rimmed by the Himalayas and lesser ranges on the north, the wedge-shaped peninsula now projects for more than 1,000 miles (1,600 kilometers) into the Indian Ocean. It is bounded by the Indian Ocean on the west and the Bay of Bengal on the east.

CHAPTER 2

According to scholar Joseph E. Schwartzberg, "The term 'subcontinent' describes what is perhaps the area's most essential feature: the remarkable degree to which it is isolated by land barriers from other major zones of human settlement."[1] This isolation limited India's external contacts, as Schwartzberg points out. At the same time, it also helped India to develop its unique culture.

India's first people occupied the Indus Valley (now in Pakistan) in about 3,000 BCE, probably arriving from Africa. Archaeologists identify them as the Harappa Culture or the Indus Valley civilization. About 2000 BCE, the Harappan society spread into the Ganges basin. The Harappans died out for reasons unknown around 1750 BCE.

Aryans from central Asia arrived to replace the Harappans and establish small kingdoms about 1500 BCE. The Mauryan Empire (c.321–185 BCE) succeeded the Aryan kingdoms. A succession of empires followed, such as the Gupta Empire (c.320–550 CE), down through 1858 when India became the crown jewel of the British Empire. It won independence from Britain in 1947, and was partitioned into two countries: the Union of India (later the Republic of India) and Pakistan. Pakistan was originally divided into West Pakistan and East Pakistan. East Pakistan became the nation of Bangladesh in 1972.

The Ganges flows through two countries. Most of its course runs across northern India, but its last 311 miles (500 km) are in Bangladesh. For part of its southward run to the Bay of Bengal it is called the Padma River. Bengal, where tigers roam, is the region encompassing the Indian state of West Bengal and Bangladesh. Of Bengal, travel writer Ilija Trojanow muses, "Bengal is one of *Ganga's* children . . . [she] has formed the plains of Bengal from her own sediments."[2] Over eons of time, the river goddess has left her imprint from the mountains to the sea.

In myth, Shiva released Ganga into the mountains in several gentle streams. Life seems to imitate fable in the geography of India's high country. To Ganga's devotees, a look at today's contour maps of the region lends a sense of authenticity to her tale. "If you look at all the rivers that flow from the Himalayas and join the Ganga as tributaries,"

comments Delhi resident Sharada Nayak, "they really look like the matted hair of Shiva; like locks of hair coming together to be braided into a gentle stream."[3] These streams are the source waters of the Ganges River.

The Ganges rises in the central Himalayas in Uttarakhand, a division of the Indian state of Uttar Pradesh. (*Himalaya* is Sanskrit for "abode of snow"; *hima*, "snow" and *alaya*, "abode.") "In India, the Himalayas have another name: Dev Bhoomi, Land of the Gods," writes Jon Nicholson. "The mountains are manifestations of all-powerful gods, and the innumerable streams and rivers fed by Himalayan glaciers are flowing forms of benevolent goddesses."[4] From an elevation of 10,319 feet (3,145 meters) at its source, the Ganges flows generally from a north-northwest to southeast direction. In its rapid descent to the valley floor,

CHAPTER 2

the river drops about 9,300 feet (2,835 meters) over a distance of only 190 miles (300 kilometers).

After its descent from the mountains, the Ganges traverses the vast Indo-Gangetic Plain and crosses into Bangladesh. Along its course, the river nurtures a flourishing basin of 416,000 square miles (669,469 square kilometers). About half of India's population of more than a billion people, along with another 25 million people in Bangladesh, lives in the basin. It is the rice bowl of both nations and provides food for a billion people.

The Ganges finally turns southward to flow into the Ganges Delta and empties into the Bay of Bengal. The Ganges Delta is formed chiefly by the Ganges and Brahmaputra rivers. It is the world's largest delta. Covering an area of some 23,000 square miles (59,000 square kilometers), it stretches along the Bay of Bengal for about 220 miles (354 kilometers). From its source to the sea, the Ganges covers a distance of 1,560 miles (2,510 kilometers). At its mouth, the river discharges thirty million gallons of water a second into the bay.

Several small streams make up the headwaters of the Ganges, but its source is usually given as Gaumukh. (Gaumukh is Sanskrit for the "cow's mouth.") It is located at the edge of the Gangotri Glacier. There the milky meltwaters appear from the ice walls. Thus the Bhagirathi River is said to flow out of the cow's mouth. To author and Ganges traveler Julian Crandall Hollick, the name appears to be a misnomer. "Nothing here resembles a cow's mouth," he writes, "there's just a glacier and a stream about twenty-five feet wide and about fifteen inches deep."[5]

Other rivers claiming to be the source of the Ganges include the Alaknandra, Mandakini, Dhauliganga, and Pindar. But the Bhagirathi remains the popular choice as the sacred river's origin. And as if to confirm Ganga's myth, the Ganges once again takes the name Bhagirathi at its other end in the plains of Bengal.

King Asoka of the Mauryan Empire

Asoka

Many scholars regard Asoka (also spelled *Ashoka*) as one of India's greatest rulers. In about 272 BCE, he became the third king of the Mauryan Empire (c.321–185 BCE). At that time, his empire—the first in India's history—comprised most of the Indian subcontinent. Only the kingdom of Kalinga on the Bay of Bengal and parts of the south fell outside his sway.

In the eighth year of his reign, Asoka waged a victorious but bloody campaign against Kalinga (now the Indian state of Orissa). After his triumph, he renounced violence and converted to Buddhism. He replaced the policy of conquest by force with one of conquest by *dharma*, the principles of right life (righteousness). Asoka spread his principles across his empire by inscribing "Edicts" upon rocks, pillars, and the walls of caves.

Asoka's First Pillar Edict is typical of his teachings. It states, in part: "This world and the other are hard to gain without great love of Righteousness, great self-examination, great obedience, great circumspection [caution], great effort. . . . For this is my rule—to govern by Righteousness."[6] As king, he practiced the Buddhist virtues of compassion and nonviolence known as *ahimsa*. He prohibited the sacrifice of animals in the capital, pardoned criminals, and constructed civic conveniences such as roads, water-storage tanks, and rest-houses.

"Though Buddhism as a distinct sect declined in India after Asoka's rule," noted author A. L. Basham, "he did much to make it part of the Indian way of life and to speed the incorporation of the ideas of duty and nonviolence into Hinduism."[7]

Mustard fields along the Ganges near the Himalayas

CHAPTER 3

The Himalayan Zone

"I think understanding Ganga as three distinct rivers is helpful in trying to solve many of the river's long-term environmental problems," asserts Julian Crandall Hollick, "because each section seems to require its own solution."[1] Hollick once traversed the entire length of the Ganges, so he writes with firsthand experience and authority. Most scientists agree with him. They divide the river's length into three distinct geologic and climatic zones: the Himalayan, the Gangetic Plain, and the Delta.

The Himalayan Zone is the shortest and most geographically spectacular of the three zones. It lies along the southern slopes of the Himalayan mountain range near the Tibetan border. The Ganges rises here among the jagged, snow-capped mountains. For the first 190 miles (300 km) of its journey to the sea, the river cascades over a series of icy waterfalls and cuts through a breathtaking array of deep gorges. After navigating one final gorge, it breaks out of the mountains and onto the Plain at the city of Haridwar.

CHAPTER 3

The Ganges cascades over an icy waterfall and carves its way through a rugged Himalayan gorge, as the sacred river plunges out of the mountains on its way to the Gangetic Plain.

Along its winding path to the valley floor, the Ganges passes several towns of historical and religious interest. Gangotri, where the goddess Ganga touched earth for the first time, is one of the most sacred places in all India. Located high in the Garhwal region, this mountain village nestles into a deep gorge surrounded by a forest of pines. A white granite temple dedicated to Ganga stands on the banks of the Bhagirathi. "Nearby is a spectacular 30-meter-high (100-foot-high) waterfall," writes Jon Nicholson, "which is venerated as an earthly reminder of Ganga's tumultuous descent and marks out Gangotri as the place where Heaven and Earth come together."[2]

Each summer, hundreds of thousands of Hindus head into the Garhwal Himalayas on a pilgrimage known as the Char Dham Yatra. Their route includes four stops. Shrines at Gangotri, Yamunotri, Kedarnath, and Badrinath mark the headwaters of the Bhagirathi, Yamuna, the Mandakini, and the Alaknanda rivers, respectively.

The Himalayan Zone

Kedarnath and Badrinath attract further devotees as the respective abodes of the gods Shiva and Vishnu. But Gangotri remains the ultimate destination for most devout pilgrims.

Yet all is not perfect in this scenic mountain setting. "Parts of this small town are concreted over with ugliness," notes Ilija Trojanow. "A little *Shiva* stands caged, looking forlorn behind gigantic bars like a prisoner arrested on false charges. Ten steps lead to his cell."[3] The "imprisoned" Shiva perhaps foretells of the culture of contrasts to be found all along the course of the Ganges.

Wildlife in the Himalayan Zone includes musk deer, snow leopards, and their favorite prey, the horned bharal, or blue sheep. The bharal is not a sheep at all but rather a goat antelope. Yellow-billed choughs fly free and thrive in the high altitude. Himalayan pikas, short-eared members of the rabbit family with short hind legs, keep a watchful eye out for the regional predators: weasels, foxes, bears, and hawks. Hanuman langurs ("mountain monkeys") with thick coats venture as high as 14,760 feet (4,500 meters). Some think their lofty presence may have led to tales of the fabled yeti—the Abominable Snowman.

Langur monkey

CHAPTER 3

Tehri Dam

From Yamunotri, the Bhagirathi twists down through terraced fields in varying shades of green to the town of Tehri (or New Tehri). The river drops more than 5,000 feet (1,529 meters) in its precipitous descent. Tehri stands at the confluence of the Bhagirathi and Bhilangna rivers. Construction of a dam on an earthquake site there drew great criticism from environmental groups and locals. And it forced the relocation of 100,000 people.

The Tehri Dam completed Phase 1 of construction and opened in 2006. It formed a reservoir for irrigation, municipal water supply, and the generation of 1,000 megawatts of hydroelectricity. Two more phases with additional capacity are to follow. Critics call the dam "a form of sacrilege, obstructing the inexorable current of a holy river that symbolizes the cosmos."[4] Local folks wonder what will happen to the silt buildup behind the dam with nowhere to dump it. Only time will provide answers to their concerns.

Meanwhile, the silt-brown Bhagirathi rolls on to its meeting with the slick green Alaknanda at Devprayag at a junction called "God's confluence." Confluences, called *prayags,* are considered holy places. They appear all along the river. Inevitably, they include temples and bathing *ghats* (steps leading down to the river) for devout bathers.

FAST FACTS

- Levels of fecal coliform (E. coli from human waste) in the Ganges River near Varanasi are more than a hundred times the official Indian government limit.
- Pollution in the Ganges threatens not only humans, but also more than 140 fish species, 90 amphibian species, and the endangered Ganges river dolphin.
- The Ganges is the longest river in India.
- The Ganges drainage basin covers parts of four countries—India, Bangladesh, Nepal, and China.
- Human development, mostly agriculture, has replaced nearly all of the original natural vegetation of the Ganges basin.
- The endangered Ganges river dolphin is said to represent the purity of the holy Ganga, as it can only survive in pure and fresh water.
- Alexander the Great believed that the Ganges formed the outermost boundary of the earth.
- About 20,000 people die from snakebite each year in India, mostly on the Gangetic Plain.
- The ancient city of Varanasi (formerly Benares) is one of the world's oldest cities, dating back more than 6,000 years.
- The Sundarbans wilderness supports somewhere between 300 and 600 tigers, possibly the world's largest tiger population.
- As many as 40,000 bodies are cremated each year at Varanasi.

CHAPTER 3

One of many bridges crossing the river

"A suspended bridge leads to a small town clambering up a steep incline," writes Ilija Trojanow. "The *ghat* at the confluence is supposed to form the outline of India, according to a travel guide."[5] At Devprayag, 124 miles (200 kilometers) downstream from Gangotri, the river officially becomes the Ganges. Water drawn from the river there can now properly be called *Gangajal* (holy water from the Ganges).

Hindus believe Gangajal comes straight from heaven and can cleanse both body and spirit. They trust in its purifying qualities even though the Ganges has become the world's fifth most-polluted river. Ilija Trojanow questioned how Hindus can allow it to become so polluted. Govind Makhanwala, a resident of Kanpur, supplied this answer: "We pollute the Ganges, because she falls under the responsibility of the gods, not us."[6]

Beyond Devprayag, the river knifes through several more deep gorges. This is the southern foothill region of the Himalayas called the Shivalik. Rolling hills run roughly east to west at an elevation of about 3,280 feet (1000 meters). Seasonal monsoons nurture thick forests of teak and bamboo, and agriculture has begun to flourish. From the foothills to Haridwar, the Ganges drops down to an elevation of 1,030 feet (314 meters) to arrive at the gateway to the plains.

Char Dham Yatra

Yamuna at Yamuntori

Mythology steeped in religion pervades every aspect of daily life in the Himalayan Zone. According to the *Mahabharata,* the gods sacrifice on the Himalayan summits. Meru, the mythological mountain of gold, towers above the rest. Brahma's city of gold perches on its summit. Both Hindus and Buddhists recognize Meru as the center, or axis, of the world. It follows that four of Hinduism's most sacred places are located in the mountains and are visited each year by pilgrims.

These sacred places are Yamunotri, Gangotri, Badrinath, and Kedarnath. The pilgrimage is called the Char Dham Yatra. (*char dham* means "the four abodes or seats"; *yatra,* "pilgrimage"). Traditionally, this yatra is made from west to east. Thus it begins in Yamunotri, the source of the sacred river Yamuna.

A temple at Yamunotri is dedicated to the goddess Yamuna, the sister of Yama, the God of Death. Pilgrims seek her blessings and salvation from an agonizing death. Experiencing the pious atmosphere and natural beauty of Gangotri is likened to being in heaven with the gods. For adventurous visitors, the town's rugged setting also offers such outdoor sports as rafting and trekking. Badnirath (from *badri,* meaning "berry") is one of the most respected Hindu shrines in India dedicated to Lord Vishnu. The temple here contains fifteen idols of Lord Vishnu, Lord Shiva, Parvati (Shiva's wife), and Garuda (a mythical bird-like creature said to be Vishnu's mount). Kednarath is the remotest of the four sites. Its temple is dedicated to Lord Shiva. Pilgrims are said to find divine peace and tranquility in Kedarnath and leave under its mesmerizing spell.

Haridwar, India marks the site where the Ganges of the Himalayas becomes the Ganges of the North Indian Plain.

CHAPTER 4

The Gangetic Plain

The 1,200-mile-long (1,931 kilometers) Indo-Gangetic Plain—or simply the Gangetic Plain—is the longest of the three geologic and climatic zones. The Ganges enters the Plain at Haridwar. Continuing on a southeasterly course, the river flows through Kanpur and Allahabad. It then turns roughly eastward until it reaches the Farakka Dam. The dam (or barrage) lies about 12 miles from India's border with Bangladesh.

Along its course across northern India, the Ganges forms a fertile basin that lies south of, and parallel to, the Himalayas. This basin varies in width from under a mile to more than 250 miles (402 kilometers). Water from the river and its tributaries sustains life in the world's most densely populated region. The Ganges leaves Haridwar at an elevation of about 1,000 feet (305 meters) and gradually descends to at an elevation of about 250 feet (76 meters) at the Farakka Dam.

Near the plains of Haridwar, the forests of the Corbett National Park and Rajaji National Park

Tigers bathe in the waters of Corbett National Park.

The Gangetic Plain

provide refuge to some of India's most intriguing wild animals—tigers, elephants, sloth bears, and peacocks. Open grasslands along the river give home to herds of chittal (or spotted deer), hog deer, and sambar (Asian deer). The Ramganga, a tributary of the Ganges, attracts Indian elephants looking for water. And predators line its banks, notably the long-snouted gharial (a fish-eating crocodile), and the mugger crocodile.

Haridwar, whose name means "gateway of the gods," is also the threshold to the Gangetic Plain. Legend has it that a drop of *amrit*, the nectar of immortality, once fell in Haridwar. (Amrit is Sanskrit for "ambrosia.") The elixir's promise of life everlasting made Haridwar one of Hinduism's seven holiest cities. Thousands of people gather at the city's bathing ghats each night to make offerings to Ganga and seek her blessings in an *aarti* (evening ritual). Vishnu is said to have left his footprint there. Every twelve years, a large bathing ceremony called the Kumbh Mela ("Pot Fair") draws millions to the city.

Kumbh Mela

CHAPTER 4

On a more secular note, Haridwar is the site of one of only two major dams on the Ganges (the other being at Farakka). "A huge barrage has allowed engineers to divert a lot of water sideways towards the bathing ghats to satisfy religious sentiments,"[1] writes Julian Crandall Hollick. (Technically, a barrage merely diverts the flow of water through gates, whereas a dam stores water in a reservoir.) After the river passes the ghats, it divides. One part flows into the 400-mile-long (644 kilometers) Ganga Canal for irrigation; the other, back into the Ganges and onto the Plain.

The Ganges has already left a dramatic imprint on its Himalayan setting. "But it now takes on a very different character—wide, sluggish, and muddy—and begins to have a much wider influence on Indian life both physically and spiritually," declares Jon Nicholson. "No longer is the Ganges just the Daughter of the Mountains. She has become Ganga Ma—Mother Ganga."[2]

One-twelfth of the world's population lives on the Gangetic Plain. Civilizations, religions, and empires have risen and fallen along the banks of Mother Ganges. Life is hard in the mountains. "Here on the plain it is a different story," notes travel writer Aldo Pavan. "The hard work is the same, but multiplied by infinity: cars, rickshaws, noise, horns blaring, cows, coloured saris. People. Hordes and hordes of people."[3] And stifling summer temperatures at a norm of 104° F (40° C). Such is life on the Plain, where hordes of people seek relief in the cooling waters of Ganga Ma.

Beyond Haridwar and past the confluence of the Ramganga, the Ganges flows by Kanpur. "Ganga at Kanpur is dirty, unappetizing and synonymous with pollution in everyone's eyes, including most of Kanpur's own citizens,"[4] asserts writer Julian Crandall Hollick. Kanpur is the second-largest industrial city on the river. Its factories draw water for their needs from the river and return poisonous waste water. Raw sewage adds to the contamination. Water-related diseases such as hepatitis abound there and await effective efforts to control the pollution. Until then, the people just wait and go about their lives.

The Gangetic Plain

The great fort built by Emperor Akbar in the 16th century lies to the east of Allahabad (also known as Prayag) just above the confluence of the Yamuna and Ganges rivers. It contains the palace of the Mughal governors, other residences, and the ancient pillar of King Asoka.

One hundred and twenty-four miles (200 kilometers) downriver, the Yamuna merges with the Ganges at Allahabad. The Yamuna—larger than Ganga at this point—delivers a large transfusion of fresh water that carries on down to Varanasi. Allahabad, another holy city, was under Muslim rule from 1194 to 1801. At that time it came under British rule and was the the scene of a serious Indian mutiny in 1857.

At Varanasi (or Benares), one of India's oldest and holiest cities, the Ganges flows north. Varanasi is the city of Shiva on earth. It lies about halfway along the river's course. Lord Shiva has promised release from the endless cycle of birth and death—the cycle of life—to anyone dying in Varanasi. During the *aarti* (evening ritual), devotees immerse themselves in the Ganges and set candles afloat in small baskets as offerings to the gods.

Once clear of Varanasi, the Ganges flows across the state of Uttar Pradesh to the city of Patna and on to Rajmahal in the state of Bihar. Several more tributaries add to the river's surge—the Gomati, Ghaghara,

CHAPTER 4

A camel driver and his dromedary stand in the shallow waters of the Yamuna in the shadow of the Taj Majal. The famous shrine was built by Mughal emperor Shah Jahan in memory of his wife, Mumtaz Mahal, who died in 1631.

and Gandaki on its left bank, and the Sone on its right. Everywhere across the Plain, travelers can see and feel the influence of the British Raj (rule). Patna once served as the capital of the Mauryan dynasty and later as the center of British operations in the Ganges basin.

Rajmahal stands on the Gange's southern bank on the vast Deccan Plateau, north of the Farakka Dam. Just above the dam—a source of ongoing trouble between India and Bangladesh—the river drops down for its final run to the sea in the delta.

British Raj

Gandhi

For many Westerners, the most interesting era in India's history is the time of the British *Raj*. (Raj is Hindi for "rule.") Officially, the period of the Raj started in 1858 and lasted until 1947. But the British presence in India began much earlier. It began with trade.

On the last day of the year 1600, Queen Elizabeth I of England granted a royal charter to the British East India Company. It authorized the company to carry out trade in the Far East. Company trading ships began to arrive in India in 1608. In 1615, King James I sent an ambassador to the ruling Mughal (Muslim) dynasty in India. Their meeting resulted in a commercial treaty between the two nations. It authorized East India Company traders to set up trading posts or "factories" in return for goods from Europe.

In 1670, under a grant from King Charles I, the East India Company acquired territory in parts of India. It raised an army, minted its own money, and exercised legal jurisdiction over the areas it controlled. In effect, the company's commercial enterprise evolved into a "nation" within a nation. British presence on the Indian subcontinent took root over the next century.

In 1857, Indian troops (sepoys) in the service of the company rebelled against British rule. The revolt was called the Indian (or Sepoy) Mutiny. It ended in a defeat for the Indians. Afterward, the British government established direct rule in India—the *Raj*. British rule lasted until India gained its independence in 1947. India owed its hard-won independence largely to the passive resistance of Mohandas Gandhi.

Upstream at the Brahmaputra River

CHAPTER 5

The Ganges Delta

At the Farakka Dam (or Barrage), the Ganges starts on the final 200 miles (322 kilometers) of its course. Just below the dam, it fans out to form the Ganges Delta, home to two million people. This 220-mile-wide (354 kilometers) arc of land in West Bengal and Bangladesh is also known as the Ganges-Brahmaputra Delta. The Brahmaputra is another of the world's great rivers that originates in the Himalayas.

After the Brahmaputra enters Bangladesh, it is joined by the Tista. From there to its junction with the Ganges it is called the Jamuna. The Ganges and the Jamuna then unite to form the Padma in Bangladesh. Before reaching the Bay of Bengal, innumerable lesser streams branch off the Ganges-Brahmaputra system. These streams form the fan-like array making up the delta and a region known as the Sundarbans. The Sundarbans is a swamp area covering about 6,526 square miles (16,902 square kilometers). It is the habitat of what is probably the

CHAPTER 5

A family of spotted deer is frozen in time by the eye of a camera in the Sundarbans, the largest mangrove forest in the world. The swampland's unique ecosystem is made possible by the constant influx of fertile silt from the Ganges.

earth's largest remaining population of tigers and a variety of other wildlife.

Because India and Bangladesh share the delta, the issue of water rights sometimes poses problems between the two countries. In the 1950s, large ships began to experience difficulties docking at Calcutta (now Kolkata). Calcutta is connected to the ocean by the Hugli (also Hooghly) River, a channel of the Ganges. The Hugli receives most of the 4.75 billion tons of silt generated annually by the Ganges. Silt was restricting navigation.

In 1975, the Indian government opened a 7,350-feet-long (2,240 meters) barrage at Farakka. It diverted water to the Hugli from the Ganges. The force of the diverted water, along with continual dredging,

The Ganges Delta

flushed the silt downriver into the Bay of Bengal. Calcutta remained open, but Bangladesh protested.

"Bangladeshis blame the Farakka Barrage for both a lack of water during the dry season and increased flooding during the wet," notes Jon Nicholson. "They claim that, beyond the barrage, the river's flow is slowed, causing it to drop more sediment, thus raising the riverbed and making it more likely that the river will break its banks during the rainy season."[1] India and Bangladesh signed a treaty for fair and equal water rights in 1996. It seems likely, however, that water disagreements will persist long into the future.

The Indian state of West Bengal and almost all of Bangladesh are built on layers of compressed mud. Across the length and breadth of an area of 77,220 square miles (200,000 square kilometers), the lands are flat as far as the eye can see. Rivers and streams of the Ganges-Brahmaputra system constantly change their courses as sediment

After the monsoon rains end in October, the lowlands of Bangladesh dry out as winter approaches, leaving a variety of fish trapped in the mud. Villagers catch the fish with their hands or scoop them up with baskets.

buildups shift their directions. The system carries 13 million tons of sediment a day to the delta in peak flood season. That amounts to twice that of the Amazon, four times that of the Nile.

This perpetual buildup of sediment first forms sandbars, then new river banks, and eventually whole new islands called chars. People who live on these chars—from a few to thousands—are among the poorest in the delta. They live in anxious anticipation from year to year, never knowing whether their land will still exist after the next flood or shift of the river. During the monsoon (rainy) season, erosion happens fast. As much as 1,312 feet (400 meters) of riverbank have been swept away in a year.

The monsoon rains from May to October feed the Ganges-Brahmaputra system. Rainfall varies in the three zones, with August receiving anywhere from eight to twenty inches. Nowhere is the effect of the river system and monsoons more apparent than it is in Bangladesh. "To travel through Bangladesh is to experience a country

The Mangroiove Forest

where the boundaries between land and water are blurred," writes Nicholson. "Water is everywhere: in rice paddies, village ponds and the hundreds of rivers that cut through the land, all of which are offshoots or tributaries of the Ganges and Brahmaputra."[2]

The watery wilderness known as the Sundarbans (literally the "beautiful forest") lies across the delta. Shared by India and Bangladesh in respective portions of 40 and 60 percent, it is the largest mangrove forest in the world. More species of mangroves grow there than can be found anywhere else in the world. The keora, the largest, reaches a height of 65 feet (20 meters) and a girth of 10 feet (3 meters). Sundari trees—from which the name Sundarbans may derive—also grow there in large numbers. At least 245 genera and 334 plant species have been recorded in the swamplands. And a 1991 study shows many wildlife species common to the wilderness: 150 of fish, 270 of birds, 42 of mammals, 35 of reptiles, and 8 of amphibians.

Chapter 5

The king of Sundarban wildlife is the much-revered Royal Bengal Tiger. These magnificent animals can swim several miles and climb trees to survive the rising waters of seasonal rains and cyclones. Shiva, the god of destruction and regeneration, is often depicted sitting on a tiger skin.

More than anything else, the Sundarbans is known as the home of the man-eating Royal Bengal Tiger. These big cats kill between 100 and 250 people in the Sundarbans each year. "We always live in fear of being devoured,"[3] Rahal told travel writer Aldo Pavan. Rahal is a 17-year-old female resident of one of about 200 or so islands of the Sundarbans.

Ironically, some scientists speculate that the tigers acquired a taste for human prey from the many corpses deposited in the Ganges during religious rites. For now, such speculation remains a theory. Other predators include king cobras, crocodiles, sharks, and the endangered Gangetic dolphins. Danger lurks everywhere in the Sundarbans.

The outermost piece of land in the Sundarbans is the mystical island of Ganga Sagar. Its name means "river-sea." The goddess Ganga traversed half of the Indian subcontinent to arrive here. It is where she redeemed the souls of King Sagara's 60,000 sons. At Ganga Sagar, the river and the sea become one. The goddess returns to the heavens, and the wheel of life turns yet again—for Ganga is the giver of life.

Pollution Problems

Polluted Ganges

To the millions of Indians who live by the Ganges, it is the most sacred river in the world. It gives them life, and they revere it. In life, they drink its water, bathe in it, wash their clothes in it, and dump their raw sewage in it. And industrial plants and tanneries drain their toxic waste in it. At life's end, they scatter ashes of their dead on it and dump whole corpses in it. How they can both revere it and revile it presents a paradox that Westerners find hard to understand or reconcile. Many wonder how long the Ganges can survive.

In 1985, the Indian government initiated the Ganges Action Plan (GAP). The GAP aims to address the needs of those whose lives depend on the river. It does so by focusing on long-term solutions to problems stemming from ongoing abuses that degrade the river's waters. Scientists and policymakers defined a series of steps designed to clean up the river and restore life to it.

Highlights of the GAP included the immediate construction of sewage treatment plants, electric crematoria (to replace funeral pyres), and public toilets in the major cities along the river. Other measures included stricter enforcement of pollution laws, and adding 30,000 alligator snapping turtles to the river near Varanasi to feed on and eliminate the rotting corpses in the river.

These measures are helping. But local attitudes, as defined by Julian Crandall Hollick, are hard to overcome: "Ganga can always survive and purify herself, precisely because she is a goddess."[4] And that attitude is precisely the problem.

Chapter Notes

Chapter 1 The Celestial Ganga
1. Claire Krulikowski, *Moonlight on the Ganga: An Intimate Memoir of a Sacred Journey along India's River of Life* (San Francisco, California: Dabue Publishing, 2000), p. 137.
2. Jon Nicholson, *Ganges* (London: BBC Books, 2007), p. 21.
3. Aldo Pavan, *The Ganges: Along Sacred Waters* (London: Thames & Hudson, 2005), p. 15.
4. Krulikowski, p. 127.

Chapter 2 Time and the River
1. Joseph E. Schwartzberg, "Land," in *India Yesterday and Today,* edited by Clark D. Moore and David Eldredge (New York: Bantam Books, 1970), p. 1.
2. Ilija Trojanow, *Along the Ganges* (London: The Armchair Traveller at the BookHaus, 2005), p. 115.
3. Julian Crandall Hollick, *Ganga: A Journey Down the Ganges River* (Washington, DC: Island Press, 2008), p. 14.
4. Jon Nicholson, *Ganges* (London: BBC Books, 2007), p. 21.
5. Hollick, p. 34.
6. A. L. Basham, "The Mauryan Dynasty," in *India Yesterday and Today,* edited by Clark D. Moore and David Eldredge (New York: Bantam Books, 1970), pp. 27–28.
7. Ibid., p. 28.

Chapter 3 The Himalayan Zone
1. Julian Crandall Hollick, Ganga: A Journey Down the Ganges River (Washington, DC: Island Press, 2008), p. 6.
2. Jon Nicholson, *Ganges* (London: BBC Books, 2007), p. 23.
3. Ilija Trojanow, *Along the Ganges* (London. UK: The Armchair Traveller at the BookHaus, 2005), p. 11.
4. Hollick, p. 36.
5. Trojanow, p. 16.
6. Ibid., p. 50.

Chapter 4 The Gangetic Plain
1. Julian Crandall Hollick, *Ganga: A Journey Down the Ganges River* (Washington, DC: Island Press, 2008), p. 42.
2. Jon Nicholson, *Ganges* (London: BBC Books, 2007), p. 51.
3. Aldo Pavan, *The Ganges: Along Sacred Waters* (London: Thames & Hudson, 2005), p. 127.
4. Hollick, p. 69.

Chapter 5 The Ganges Delta
1. Jon Nicholson, *Ganges* (London: BBC Books, 2007), p. 126.
2. Ibid.
3. Aldo Pavan, *The Ganges: Along Sacred Waters* (London: Thames & Hudson, 2005), p. 295.
4. Julian Crandall Hollick, *Ganga: A Journey Down the Ganges River* (Washington, D.C.: Island Press, 2008), p. 9.

Works Consulted

Barter, James. *The Ganges*. Rivers of the World Series. Farmington Hills, Michigan: Lucent Books, 2003.
Hollick, Julian Crandall. *Ganga: A Journey Down the Ganges River*. Washington, D.C.: Island Press, 2008.
Krulikowski, Claire. *Moonlight on the Ganga: An Intimate Memoir of a Sacred Journey along India's River of Life*. San Francisco, California: Dabue Publishing, 2000.
Moore, Clark D., and David Eldredge (editors). *India Yesterday and Today*. New York: Bantam Books, 1970.
Newby, Eric. *Slowly Down the Ganges*. Oakland, California: Lonely Planet Publications, 1998.
Nicholson, Jon. *Ganges*. London: BBC Books, 2007.
Pavan, Aldo. *The Ganges: Along Sacred Waters*. London: Thames & Hudson, 2005.
Pollard, Michael. *The Ganges*. Great Rivers Series. Tarrytown, New York: Benchmark Books, 1998.
Thomas, Frederic C. *To the Mouths of the Ganges: An Ecological and Cultural Journey*. Norwalk, Connecticut: EastBridge, 2004.
Trojanow, Ilija. *Along the Ganges*. London: The Armchair Traveller at the BookHaus, 2005.

Further Reading

Books
Aloian, Molly. *The Ganges: India's Sacred River*. Rivers Around the World. New York: Crabtree Publishing Company, 2010.
Bowden, Rob. *Ganges*. River Journey. London: Hodder Wayland, 2007.
Lewin, Ted. *Sacred River. The Ganges of India*. Boston: Houghton Mifflin Harcourt, 2003.
Petrie, Kristin. *Ganges River Dolphins*. Edina, Minnesota: Abdo Publishing Company, 2006.
Spilsbury, Louise. *Living on the Ganges River*. Mankato, Minnesota: Heinemann-Raintree, 2008.
Spilsbury, Richard. *Settlements of the Ganges River*. Rivers Through Time Series. Mankato, Minnesota: Heinemann-Raintree, 2005.

On the Internet
Abrams, Paula. "River Ganges"
    http://www.africanwater.org/ganges.htm
Academic Kids: Ganges River
    http://academickids.com/encyclopedia/index.php/Ganges_River
Gupta, Anika. "The Holy City of Varanasi"
    http://www.smithsonianmag.com/travel/The-Holy-City-of-Varanasi.html?c=y&story=fullstory
Hammer, Joshua. "A Prayer for the Ganges"
    http://www.smithsonianmag.com/people-places/ganges-200711.html?c=y&story=fullstory
Kamat, Vikas. "The River Ganga (Ganges)"
http://www.kamatr.com/indica/rivers/ganga.htm

PHOTO CREDITS: All photos—cc-by-sa-2.0. Every effort has been made to locate all copyright holders of material used in this book. If any errors or omissions have occurred, corrections will be made in future editions of the book.

Glossary

aarti (AHR-tee)—An evening ceremony characterized by the circling of oil lamps before the divine image

ahimsa (uh-HIM-suh)—The Hindu and Buddhist doctrine of refraining from harming any living thing

amrit (AHM-rit)—Sanskrit for "ambrosia," the nectar of the gods.

avatarana (uh-vuh-TAHR-uh-nuh)—The descent of the Ganges from heaven to earth, which Hindus celebrate annually in late May or early June

barrage (BAHR-ij)—A dam placed in a watercourse to increase the depth of water or to divert it into a channel for navigation or irrigation

confluence (KAHN-floo-ents)—The place where two streams meet

dam (DAM)—A barrier preventing the flow of water or loose solid materials (as snow or soil), especially a barrier built across a watercourse for impeding the flow of water

dharma (DHAR-muh)—In Hinduism, an individual's duty fulfilled by observance or custom or law; the basic principles of cosmic or individual existence; divine law

Gangajal (GAN-guh-jal)—Sacred water from the Ganges

ghat (goht)—A broad flight of steps situated on a Hindu riverbank to provide bathers with access to the river

prayag (PRAY-ag)—Sacred places of worship at river confluences, usually with temples and bathing *ghats*

Raj (rahj)—Hindi for "rule," especially the former British rule of the Indian subcontinent.

Index

aarti 31, 33
Agni 7
ahimsa 19
Alaknandra River 18
Allahabad 9, 29, 33, 34
amrit 31
Asoka (Ashoka) 19, 33
avatarana 6, 9
Bangladesh 16, 18, 25, 29, 34, 37, 38, 39, 40, 41
Bay of Bengal 9, 15, 16, 18, 19, 37, 39
Bhagavad-Gita 13
Bhagirath 8, 9, 11
Bhagirathi River 9, 10, 18, 22, 24
Brahma 6, 7, 8
Brahmaputra River 18, 36, 37, 39, 40, 41
British East India Company 35
British Empire (Raj) 16, 34, 35
Buddha 7
Calcutta (Kolkata) 38, 39
Char Dham Yatra 22, 27
Corbett National Park 29, 30
Devprayag 24, 26
dharma 19
Dhauliganga River 18
Farakka Dam (or Barrage) 29, 32, 34, 37, 38, 39
Gandhi, Mohandas 34, 35
Ganga 5, 6, 7, 8, 9, 11, 12, 15, 16, 21, 22, 25, 31, 32, 33, 42, 43
Ganga Canal 32
Gangajal 12, 26
Ganga Sagar 9, 42
Ganges Action Plan (GAP) 43
Ganges-Brahmaputra system 37, 39, 40
Ganges Delta 18, 37, 39, 41
Ganges River 4, 5, 6, 9, 10, 11, 12, 16, 17, 18, 20, 21, 22, 25, 26, 28, 29, 31, 32, 33, 34, 37, 38, 39, 40, 41, 42, 43
Gangetic dolphin 25
Gangetic Plain (Indo-Gangetic Plain) 18, 21, 25, 31, 32, 33
Gangotri 22, 23, 26, 27
Gangotri Glacier 18
Gaumukh 18
ghat 12, 26
Haridwar 9, 21, 26, 28, 29, 32
Harappans 16

Himalayas 5, 9, 11, 14, 15, 16, 17, 20, 22, 26, 28, 29, 37
Himavat 11
Hindu(s) 5, 6, 9, 11, 12, 22, 26, 27
Hinduism 11, 13, 19
Hugli (Hooghly) River 38
India 7, 13, 14, 15, 16, 17, 19, 22, 25, 26, 27, 28, 29, 34, 35, 38, 39, 41
Indian (or Sepoy) Mutiny 35
Jamuna River 37
Kailas, Mount 8, 9
Kanpur 26, 29, 32
Kapila 7
Kumbh Mela ("Pot Fair") 31
Mahabharata 6, 7, 12, 13, 27
Mandakini River 18, 22
Mauryan Empire 16, 19, 34
monsoon 39, 40
Nehru, Jawaharlal 5
Padma River 16, 37
Pakistan 16
Patna 33, 34
prayag 34
Pindar River 18
Purana 7
Ramganga River 31, 32
Rajaji National Park 29
Rajmahal 33, 34
Ramayana 7, 13
Rig Veda (Rigveda) 13
Royal Bengal Tiger 42
Sagara 7, 8, 9
Shiva 6, 7, 8, 16, 17, 23, 27, 33, 42
Sundarbans 25, 37, 41, 42
Tehri (or New Tehri) 24
Tista River 37
Uttarakhand 17
Uttar Pradesh 17, 33
Varanasi 9, 12, 25, 33, 43
Vishnu 6, 7, 23, 27, 31
West Bengal 16, 37, 39
wildlife 23, 38, 41
Yamuna River 9, 22, 27, 33, 34

ABOUT THE AUTHOR

Earle Rice Jr. is a former senior design engineer and technical writer in the aerospace, electronic-defense, and nuclear industries. He has devoted full time to his writing since 1993 and is the author of more than 60 published books. Earle is listed in *Who's Who in America* and is a member of the Society of Children's Book Writers and Illustrators, the League of World War I Aviation Historians, the Air Force Association, and the Disabled American Veterans.